Just So Stories

The Elephant's Child

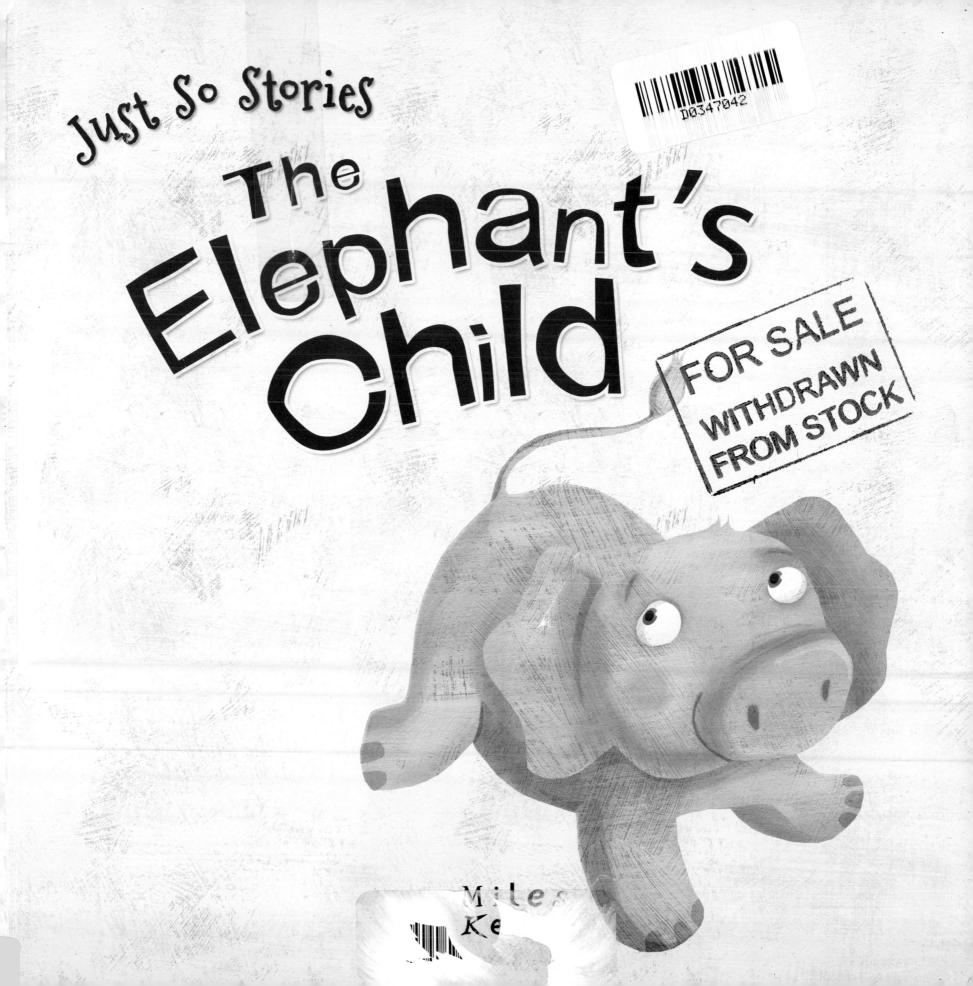

Miles
Ke

In the high and far-off times the elephant had no trunk – only a bulgy nose, as big as a boot.

He could wriggle it from side to side, but he couldn't pick anything up with it.

But there was one elephant's child who was full of 'satiable curtiosity.

That means he asked ever so many questions.

He asked his hairy uncle, the baboon, why melons tasted just so, and his uncle pinched him with his hairy paw.

He asked his tall uncle, the giraffe, what made his skin spotty, and his uncle cuffed him with his hard hoof.

He asked his broad aunt, the hippo, why her eyes were red, and his aunt splashed him with her broad hoof.

But still he was full of 'satiable curtiosity!

One day the elephant's child asked,
"What does the crocodile have for dinner?"
But all his family just said,

"HUSH!"

So the elephant's child went
to the kolokolo bird and asked,
"What does the crocodile
have for dinner?"

"Go to the banks of the
great grey-green, greasy
Limpopo River,
and find out," said the bird.

So the next morning, the 'satiable elephant's child set off to find the great grey-green, greasy Limpopo River.

"Goodbye!"

Now this 'satiable elephant's child had never seen a crocodile, and did not know what one was like.

The first creature that he found was a bi-coloured-python-rock-snake, curled round a rock.

"'Scuse me," said the elephant's child, "but have you seen such a thing as a crocodile around here? And could you tell me what he has for dinner?"

But instead of answering, the snake gave the elephant's child a sharp slap with his scalesome, flailsome tail.

Further on, the elephant's child trod on what looked like a log at the edge of the Limpopo River.

But it was really the crocodile!

"'Scuse me," said the elephant's child. "Have you seen such a thing as a crocodile around here?"

The crocodile said, "I am the crocodile."

"Then will you tell me what you have for dinner?" gasped the elephant's child.

"Come close and I'll whisper," said the crocodile.

The elephant's child put his ear to the crocodile's musky tusky mouth.

At once, the crocodile caught the elephant's child by his little nose. "Today," he said "I will begin with elephant's child!"

"Led go!" the elephant's child said, speaking through his nose, "You're hurtig be!"

Then the bi-coloured-python-rock-snake shouted, "Pull! Or you will be in the river before you can say Jack Robinson."

So the elephant's child sat back on his little haunches, and pulled, and pulled, and pulled, and his nose began to stretch.

Then the snake came and knotted himself in a double-clove-hitch round the elephant's child's hind legs. They both pulled together.

The elephant's child's nose grew *longer* and *longer!*

At last the crocodile let go of the elephant's child's nose with a plop! that you could hear for miles around.

SPLASH!

The elephant's child wrapped his poor nose in banana leaves, and hung it in the river.

"What are you doing that for?" asked the snake.

"My nose is all out of shape," said the elephant's child, "and I'm hoping it will shrink."

Then a fly landed on the elephant's child's shoulder. He lifted up his long nose and SMACKED it away.

"Ah ha!" said the snake. "You couldn't have done that with a mere-smear nose."

In the afternoon, the snake asked, "Isn't the sun hot?"

Splat!

"Yes," said the elephant's child. He schlooped up some mud from the river bank and sloshed it on his head. It made a cool mud cap, all trickly behind his ears.

"Ah ha!" said the snake again. "You couldn't have done that with a mere-smear nose."

"You're right," said the elephant's child. "And now I think I'll go home to all my dear family."

So the elephant's child went home, frisking and whisking his new long nose – which we now call a trunk.

When he wanted fruit to eat he pulled it down from a tree.

Swish!

When he felt lonely he **sang** loudly to himself down his trunk.

When flies bit him he broke off the branch of a tree and used it as a swat.

When he reached home, the elephant's child uncurled his trunk and said, "How do you do?"

"Indeed," said his hairy uncle the baboon.

"It looks very ugly," sniffed his broad aunt the hippo.

"What have you done to your nose?" asked his tall uncle the giraffe.

"But it's USEFUL," said the elephant's child. He picked up his hairy uncle the baboon, and dropped him into a thorn bush.

Then he trumpeted in the ear of his tall uncle the giraffe, and blew bubbles at his broad aunt the hippo.

The new nose was so useful that all the elephants hurried to the banks of the Limpopo River to borrow new noses from the crocodile.

Ever since then, all the elephants you will ever see – and all those you won't – have noses precisely like the trunk of the 'satiable elephant's child.